Dear Parents:

Congratulations! Your child is taking the first steps on an exciting journey. The destination? Independent reading!

STEP INTO READING® will help your child get there. The program offers five steps to reading success. Each step includes fun stories and colorful art or photographs. In addition to original fiction and books with favorite characters, there are Step into Reading Non-Fiction Readers, Phonics Readers and Boxed Sets, Sticker Readers, and Comic Readers—a complete literacy program with something to interest every child.

Learning to Read, Step by Step!

Ready to Read **Preschool–Kindergarten**
• big type and easy words • rhyme and rhythm • picture clues
For children who know the alphabet and are eager to begin reading.

Reading with Help **Preschool–Grade 1**
• basic vocabulary • short sentences • simple stories
For children who recognize familiar words and sound out new words with help.

Reading on Your Own **Grades 1–3**
• engaging characters • easy-to-follow plots • popular topics
For children who are ready to read on their own.

Reading Paragraphs **Grades 2–3**
• challenging vocabulary • short paragraphs • exciting stories
For newly independent readers who read simple sentences with confidence.

Ready for Chapters **Grades 2–4**
• chapters • longer paragraphs • full-color art
For children who want to take the plunge into chapter books but still like colorful pictures.

STEP INTO READING® is designed to give every child a successful reading experience. The grade levels are only guides; children will progress through the steps at their own speed, developing confidence in their reading.

Remember, a lifetime love of reading starts with a single step!

Copyright © 2019 Disney Enterprises, Inc. and Pixar. All rights reserved. Published in
the United States by Random House Children's Books, a division of Penguin Random House LLC,
1745 Broadway, New York, NY 10019, and in Canada by Penguin Random House Canada
Limited, Toronto, in conjunction with Disney Enterprises, Inc.

Step into Reading, Random House, and the Random House colophon are registered trademarks
of Penguin Random House LLC.

Visit us on the Web!
StepIntoReading.com
rhcbooks.com

Educators and librarians, for a variety of teaching tools, visit us at RHTeachersLibrarians.com

ISBN 978-0-7364-3983-1 (trade) — ISBN 978-0-7364-8275-2 (lib. bdg.)
ISBN 978-0-7364-3984-8 (ebook)

Printed in the United States of America   10 9 8 7 6 5 4 3 2 1

Disney · PIXAR

COCO

A Puppy for Miguel

by Melissa Lagonegro

based on an original story by
Roni Capin Rivera-Ashford and Daniel Rivera Ashford

illustrated by the Disney Storybook Art Team

Random House 🏠 New York

A hungry puppy
lives alone
on an old farm.

The puppy leaves
the farm.
He wants to find food
and make friends.

He finds a place
with lots
of leftover food.
He cannot wait to eat!

He fills his belly
with tasty food.
Then he takes a nap.

The puppy wakes up.

He meets new friends.

They run and play.

The puppy smells
something yummy.
He follows the scent.

The smell leads him

to a busy town.

He sees a lot

of food and people.

He wags his tail!

The puppy meets a nice boy named Miguel. Miguel shows him around town.

The puppy meets
a kind butcher
and a friendly teacher.
They give him
food and water.

Not everyone is kind.

A garbage man yells.

A farmer has a sharp
fence to keep the
puppy out.

Miguel's abuelita
does not like stray dogs.
She chases the puppy
away.

The puppy grows
bigger and stronger.
He and Miguel
are friends.

The dog loves spending time with Miguel. They listen to music while Miguel works.

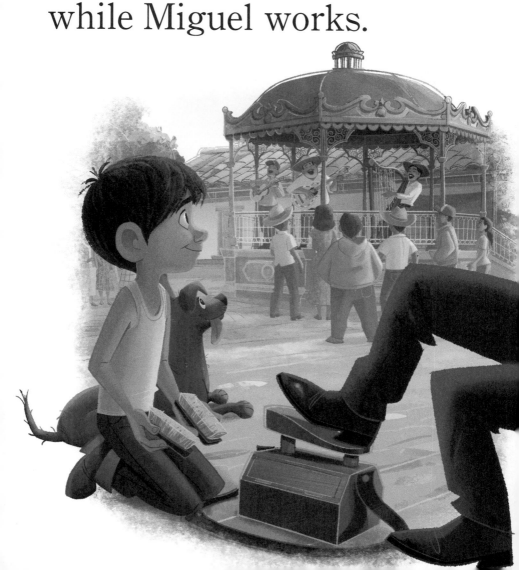

Abuelita always tries
to chase the dog away.

She throws
her shoe at him.

He runs, but he knows
he will see Miguel again.

The dog hears music.

He follows the sound.

He finds Miguel

playing his guitar!

Every time the dog
misses his friend,
he follows the music.

There is Miguel!
The friends are
always so happy
to see each other.
Miguel gives
the dog a name.
He calls him Dante.

Dante loves
his new name.
He loves his new friend
even more!